Parents and Caregivers,

Stone Arch Readers are designed to provide enjoyable reading experiences, as well as opportunities to develop vocabulary, literacy skills, and comprehension. Here are a few ways to support your beginning reader:

- Talk with your child about the ideas addressed in the story.

- Discuss each illustration, mentioning the characters, where they are, and what they are doing.

- Read with expression, pointing to each word. You may want to read the whole story through and then revisit parts of the story to ensure that the meanings of words or phrases are understood.

- Talk about why the character did what he or she did and what your child would do in that situation.

- Help your child connect with characters and events in the story.

Remember, reading with your child should be fun, not forced. Each moment spent reading with your child is a priceless investment in his or her literacy life.

Gail Saunders-Smith, Ph.D.

STONE ARCH **READERS**

are published by Stone Arch Books
A Capstone Imprint
151 Good Counsel Drive, P.O. Box 669
Mankato, Minnesota 56002
www.capstonepub.com

Library of Congress Cataloging-in-Publication Data
Suen, Anastasia.
Snow games : a Robot and Rico story / by Anastasia Suen ; illustrated by
Mike Laughead.
p. cm. — (Stone Arch readers)
ISBN 978-1-4342-1869-8 (library binding)
ISBN 978-1-4342-2302-9 (pbk.)
[1. Snow—Fiction. 2. Robots—Fiction.] I. Laughead, Mike, ill. II. Title.
PZ7.S94343Sn 2010
[E]—dc22
2009034210

Summary: Robot and Rico use sleds, skiis, tubes, and more to enjoy the new snow.

Art Director: Bob Lentz
Graphic Designer: Hilary Wacholz

Reading Consultants:
Gail Saunders-Smith, Ph.D.
Melinda Melton Crow, M.Ed.
Laurie K. Holland, Media Specialist

SNOW GAMES

BY ANASTASIA SUEN

ILLUSTRATED BY MIKE LAUGHEAD

A ROBOT AND RICO STORY

STONE ARCH BOOKS
a capstone imprint

This is ROBOT.
Robot has lots of tools.

He uses the tools to help his
best friend, Rico.

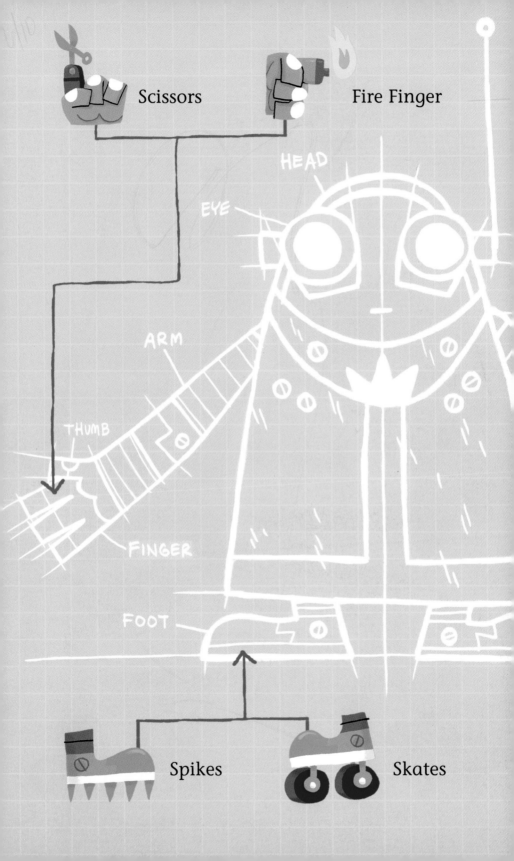

Rico digs and digs and digs.

"What are you doing?" asks Robot.

"I'm getting my winter stuff ready," says Rico.

"Why?" asks Robot. "There isn't any snow yet."

"I want to be ready," says Rico.

"Now what do we do?" asks Robot.

"We wait for the snow," says Rico.

They wait. And wait. And wait.

They wake up and see lots of snow.

"Race you to the top of the hill," says Rico.

"I won!" says Rico.

"I guess you did," says Robot.

"Let's go sledding first," says Robot.

"Race you to the bottom!" says Rico.

"I won!" says Rico.

"I guess you did," says Robot.
"Back up the hill."

"What next?" asks Robot.

"Tubing," says Rico. "Race you
to the bottom!"

"I won!" says Rico.

"I guess you did," says Robot.
"Back up the hill."

"Grab the snowboards," says Robot.

"Race you to the bottom!" says Rico.

"I won!" says Rico.

"I guess you did," says Robot.
"Back up the hill."

"What's left?" asks Robot.

"The skis!" says Rico.

"Let me guess," says Robot. "You want to race."

"See you at the bottom!" says Rico.

"Now what?" asks Robot.
"We've used everything."

"There's nothing left to do,"
says Rico.

"There is one thing left to do,"
says Robot. "Follow me."

When he pushes a button,
Robot turns into a bobsled.

"Wow!" says Rico.

"Jump on," says Robot.

Together, Robot and Rico race
down the hill.

"We don't need all that stuff,"
says Robot.

"Not when we have each other,"
says Rico.

"I guess we both won," says Robot.

"I guess we did," says Rico.

STORY WORDS

winter

race

won

guess

sledding

tubing

snowboards

skis

bobsled

Total Word Count: 283

One robot. One boy. One crazy fun friendship! Read all the Robot and Rico adventures!